For my Parents

Text and illustrations by Hendrik Jonas
Originally published under the titel: Eine Vogelhochzeit
© 2018 by Tulipan Verlag GmbH, Munich, Germany
www.tulipan.de
© for the English edition: 2019, Prestel Verlag,
Munich · London · New York
A member of Verlagsgruppe Random House GmbH
Neumarkter Strasse 28 · 81673 Munich

Prestel Publishing Ltd.
14-17 Wells Street
London W1T 3PD

Prestel Publishing
900 Broadway, Suite 603
New York, NY 10003

Library of Congress Control Number: 2018949225
A CIP catalogue record for this book is available
from the British Library.

Translated from German by Paul Kelly
Copyediting: Brad Finger
Production management: Susanne Hermann
Typesetting: textum GmbH, Feldafing
Printing and binding: DZS Grafik d.o.o.

Verlagsgruppe Random House FSC® N001967

Printed in Slovenia

ISBN 978-3-7913-7379-9
www.prestel.com

Hendrik Jonas

The Song of Spring

Prestel

Munich · London · New York

As spring approaches, the birds begin to sing, whistle, and chirp so they can attract some friends.

When Mr. Blackbird sings the 'blackbird song',
Mrs. Blackbird comes flying by.

It's the same with robins and
with all the other birds, too.

With this little bird, however, it was different. He could not remember his song of spring.

But because he wanted
to find a friend, he hastily
opened his beak one day
and shrieked:

woof

'Woof, woof', answered the dog
and wagged its tail.

'That wasn't quite right',
thought the little bird.
'Have another go', said the dog.
The little bird cried out:

oink

'Oops!', said the little bird.
'But you are not a bird!'
'No', said the pig.
'I am a pig. Oink, oink.'

The little bird thought a bit.
The pig and the dog had not
been much help at all.
So he shouted:

moo

'Cooee!', said the cow and stared
at the bird with its great big eyes.
The little bird had to sit down,
not least because of the huge shock.

The cow was mooing,

the dog was barking,

the pig was grunting.

The little bird could
not concentrate.

meow

'Oh!', said the little bird and
slid back a little on his branch.
The cat purred softly and said:
'Hello, little one.'

The pig, the dog, the cow, and the cat scrambled about in the tree. The bird thought hard and then sheepishly cried out:

meh?

'Did you just say: meh?', enquired the goat.
'It came out wrong', said the little bird, and
he blushed a lot.

'Now I have it', cried the little bird.
Nervously the goat, the pig, the cow,
the cat, and the dog looked on.

The bird chirped:

hee-
haw

'Well, you sang that beautifully', said the friendly donkey. 'I am looking for a bird friend', moaned the little bird quite sadly. 'But it is not working out.'

So what now? The donkey, the goat, the pig, the cat, the dog, and the cow looked quizzically at the little bird. At last, he said: 'I cannot think of anything.'

Akward silence.
Pawing the ground.
Ear wiggling.
Horn scratching.

Suddenly there was
a deafening sound:

parp!

What was THAT?

'Hello', said a pretty girl bird.
'I have come from very far away,
and I am looking for a friend.
But I cannot find one.
Could you help me?'

cried the pig and the dog
and the donkey and the goat
and the cow and the cat.
The little bird was very happy.

woof

meow

cheep-
cheep

roar

hee-haw

And that is how the little bird,
who could not remember the
song of spring, found not only
one but many friends.